BRER RABBIT AND THE SWING

Mr Man catches Brer Rabbit stealing carrots from his garden. He swings Brer Rabbit up by the ears and puts him in a hutch closely guarded by his little girl. Brer Rabbit watches the little girl swinging up and down on her swing and a clever plan for escape comes into his mind. But can he persuade Mr Man to let him have a turn on the swing?

A collection of the popular Brer Rabbit stories written by Enid Blyton

ENID BLYTON

BRER RABBIT and the Swing

Illustrated Val Biro

KNIGHT BOOKS
Hodder and Stoughton

ISBN 0 340 22162 3

All rights reserved
Illustrations copyright © 1977 Hodder and Stoughton Ltd
First published in 1953 by Latimer House Limited
This edition published in 1977

Printed and bound in Great Britain in Knight Books
for Hodder and Stoughton Children's Books, a division of
Hodder and Stoughton Ltd, Arlen House,
Salisbury Road, Leicester by
Cox & Wyman Ltd, London, Reading and Fakenham

This book is sold subject to the condition that it shall not by way of trade or otherwise be lent, re-sold, hired out or otherwise circulated without the publisher's prior consent in any form of binding or cover other than that in which this is published and without a similar condition including this condition being imposed on the subsequent purchaser

Contents

Brer Rabbit and the swing

Once, when Brer Rabbit was nibbling carrots in Mr Man's garden, Mr Man came along and caught him neatly by the ears. He swung him up into the air and cried, 'Ha! Here's the fellow that eats my greens! Here's the fellow that nibbles my carrots!'

'Please, sir, I'll never do it again,' squealed Brer Rabbit, his nose trembling up and down with fright.

'You're right there – you never will!' said Mr Man, with a grin, and he tucked Brer Rabbit under his arm and walked off down the garden with him.

Soon he came to where his little girl was swinging up and down on her swing. She stopped swinging and called out, 'What have you got, Daddy?'

'I've got the fellow that eats my greens!' said Mr Man, and he swung Brer Rabbit by his ears again. Brer Rabbit hated it. Just then a boy in the next field shouted to Mr Man.

'Hey! Can you come here a minute, sir?'

'Coming!' shouted Mr Man. He stuffed poor Brer Rabbit into a wooden hutch nearby and spoke to his little girl. 'Now listen to me – whatever you do, don't let Brer Rabbit out of that hutch. No matter what he says to you, don't you let him out. See?'

'I promise I won't, Daddy,' said the little girl, and she went on swinging. Brer Rabbit heard the door of the hutch slammed, and saw Mr Man run off to the next field.

'I'll be back in five minutes,' said Mr Man, 'and then Brer Rabbit will be in a bad way!'

As soon as Mr Man was gone, Brer Rabbit spoke to the little girl.

'That's a fine swing you've got, little girl!' he said.

'Yes,' she said. 'My Daddy made it for me. It goes very, very high – so high that I can see right over the wall into the next field, where there are lots of rabbit-burrows.'

'Are there really?' sighed Brer Rabbit, wishing and wishing that he was down a burrow. 'Oh, little girl, wouldn't I just love a swing on your swing! Do let me have a turn. You could push me

very high and I wouldn't be afraid.'

'My Daddy said I mustn't let you out of the hutch,' said the little girl, swinging to and fro.

'But, little girl, it wouldn't matter if you let me have a swing,' said Brer Rabbit. 'I could jump back into the hutch as soon as your Daddy came back.'

'I dare say you could,' said the little girl. 'But I promised Daddy I wouldn't let you out of the hutch.'

'Little girl, I think you are very selfish,' said Brer Rabbit, turning up his nose at her. 'You want your swing all to yourself, that's why you won't let *me* have a turn. And I've never, never had a swing in my life. I do think you might let me.'

'I told Daddy I wouldn't let you out of the hutch,' said the little girl. 'But I tell you what I will do for you, Brer Rabbit, just to show you that I am *not* selfish about my swing – I'll ask my Daddy to let you have a turn when he comes back.'

'All right,' said Brer Rabbit. 'But he won't let me. You'll see.'

Just then Mr Man came back, and he was pleased to see Brer Rabbit still in the hutch.

'You're a good little girl,' he said to his small daughter. 'You have kept guard on that wicked rabbit very well. What shall I give you for a reward?'

'Oh, Daddy, will you let the rabbit have a turn on my swing?' asked the little girl eagerly. 'He says he has never been on a swing. Maybe it's the last thing he'll ever do, so you might let him do it – just to please me!'

'Well,' said Mr Man, rather doubtfully, 'I'll only let him if *I* put him on the swing and *I* take him off – or he may skip away!'

'Oh, please, Mr Man, you can put me on and take me off yourself,' cried out Brer Rabbit in a pleased voice. 'Oh, you are very kind to let me have a swing! If *you* put me on and take me off, I can't skip away, can I?'

Mr Man opened the hutch door and took out Brer Rabbit by the ears. He set him on the swing and then began to push him high.

'Oh, higher still, higher still!' cried Brer Rabbit in a delighted voice. 'This is lovely!'

The little girl pushed Brer Rabbit higher and higher. He swung to and fro, his whiskers waving as he went. At last he swung so high that he could see right over the wall and into the next field.

And then old Brer Rabbit jumped! Yes – he waited till the swing was very high, almost over the wall, and then he leapt right off it, over the wall, into a bramble bush, and before anyone could say 'Jack Robinson!' he was gone, and the swing was empty.

'He's gone!' cried Mr Man. 'Where did he go?

Quick! Look for him!'

But though they looked and looked they didn't find old Brer Rabbit. He couldn't have jumped over that wall if he hadn't been swung so high – and he was down a burrow giggling to think of Mr Man's face when he suddenly saw that the swing was empty!

'It's a pity Mr Man didn't feel in my pockets!' said Brer Rabbit, and he took out three large carrots and began to nibble them. 'Poor Mr Man – he's no match for Brer Rabbit!'

Brer Rabbit's sausages

ONCE it happened that Brer Rabbit went to the butcher's and bought a fine string of fat sausages. He was mighty pleased with them, and went home through the woods, lippitty-clippitty, singing a little song.

And who should meet him but Brer Fox and Brer Bear, both looking mighty glum, for they had been fishing and hadn't caught so much as a minnow.

Brer Rabbit ran right into them, and they held him fast.

'Now, now, what are you running away from?' said Brer Fox. 'Have you been stealing those sausages?'

'Indeed I haven't,' said Brer Rabbit. 'I'm an honest fellow, I am! I don't steal sausages.'

'Brer Bear, don't you think we ought to take these sausages away from him?' said Brer Fox, winking at Brer Bear. 'We'd better take them back to the butcher and see if Brer Rabbit has paid for them.'

'Of course I've paid for them,' said Brer Rabbit angrily. But he was glad to escape from Brer Fox and Brer Bear, even if it meant leaving his beautiful sausages behind. He edged away from them – and then suddenly ran under a bush and down a hole.

'Ho ho!' laughed Brer Fox. 'We've caught no fish, Brer Bear – but we've caught some fine sausages instead! Come along – we'll go to your house and cook them.'

Well, Brer Rabbit heard what was said and he was very angry. He skipped out of the hole as soon as he saw Brer Fox and Brer Bear going off – and he followed behind them all the way.

They went into Brer Bear's house. Brer Bear lighted a fire to cook the sausages, and Brer Rabbit saw the smoke coming out of the chimney. He sat by the gate and thought hard.

Outside the front door stood the fishing-rods and lines, left there by Brer Bear and Brer Fox. Brer Rabbit grinned a little and smacked his leg softly. If he didn't get back those sausages, his name wasn't Brer Rabbit!

He slipped along to the front door. He took

one of the fishing-rods. He crept round to the back and stood on the big water-butt there. He climbed from that on to the roof and scrambled quietly up to the chimney that was smoking.

Brer Rabbit put his head down it and sniffed. Yes – he could smell those sausages cooking all right! He set a hook on the end of the fishing-line and unwound it. He dropped the hook gently down the chimney till it stopped falling, and he knew it had reached the frying-pan.

Brer Bear had put the sausages into the pan of fat without cutting the string that bound them to one another. There they lay in the pan, a nice string of sizzling sausages! Brer Bear and Brer Fox were laying the table.

'A plate for you and a plate for me,' Brer Rabbit heard Brer Bear say. He jerked his line about, trying to catch the hook into the string of sausages – and at last it caught!

Brer Rabbit grinned. He wound up the line. The sausages came up the chimney, getting a bit sooty as they went. But Brer Rabbit didn't mind that. Oh no – a little soot was nothing to him!

The sausages came right out of the chimney. They were mighty hot, so Brer Rabbit took a clean handkerchief from his pocket and spread it on the roof. He put the sizzling sausages there and waited for them to cool. They were just nicely cooked.

He stood up and cocked one ear over the chimney. 'One mug for you, one mug for me,' he heard Brer Bear say. And then he heard an angry yell.

'Hie, Brer Fox! Where are those sausages? They're not in the pan!'

There was a moment's surprised silence. Then

Brer Fox spoke up. '*You've* taken those sausages, Brer Bear. I haven't touched them, I know that. You've taken them out of the pan when I wasn't looking. Where are they?'

'That's what *I* should like to know!' cried Brer Bear angrily. 'You just put them back in the pan, Brer Fox, or I'll squeeze you to bits!'

Brer Fox shouted in rage – and then Brer Rabbit heard the two of them rushing round and round the kitchen trying to hit one another.

Crash! Down went a kettle! Clang! Down went three saucepans! Thud! Over went a chair! Smash! The kitchen table overturned. My, there was a fine old to-do in Brer Bear's kitchen that day! Brer Rabbit got so excited that he did a little dance up there on the roof and nearly fell off.

Then out rushed Brer Fox, with Brer Bear after him. They ran down the path and into the woods, both yelling and howling fit to wake a hundred sleepers.

Brer Rabbit did enjoy it all. He sat up there on the roof chewing those sausages, and grinning to himself.

And when at last the two of them came back from the woods, hungry, tired, and sore, what

did they see but Brer Rabbit sitting up on the roof waving to them.

'I've saved you the sausage skins!' shouted Brer Rabbit, and he threw them at Brer Bear, smack! Then down he jumped to the water-butt and set off home as fast as his legs could carry him – but every now and again he stopped and rolled on the ground with laughter. Oh, he's a comic fellow is Brer Rabbit, no doubt about that!

Poor Old Brer Bear

ONCE it happened that Brer Rabbit was chased so hard by Brer Fox that he just had to climb up a tree. Now this was mighty difficult for him, and he wouldn't have done it at all if there had been a hole near, but there wasn't.

So up he scrabbled, panting and puffing, and sat up on a high branch, looking down at Brer Fox. Brer Fox wasn't good at climbing trees, so he sat at the foot of the tree and scowled.

'Come on down, Brer Rabbit,' he said, 'come on down.'

'I can't,' said Brer Rabbit. 'It was difficult enough to get up – but I'm mighty certain I'd break my neck if I jumped down.'

Brer Fox looked up at the high branch on which Brer Rabbit sat, and he knew that Brer Rabbit spoke the truth. He couldn't get down!

'Well, I'm a-going to get my axe, Brer Rabbit,' said Brer Fox. 'I'm going to chop down this tree and get you this time! You can just stay there till

I come back! Then down you'll come with the tree, smack!'

Brer Fox ran off. Brer Rabbit sat up in the tree, looking blue. Should he drop down and hope he would be hurt? Should he stay where he was and hope to escape when the tree came down? He looked down at the ground. No – it was too far away, that was certain.

Just then Brer Rabbit heard the sound of someone lumbering through the wood, singing a deep, growly song.

'That's Brer Bear,' thought Brer Rabbit, peering through the leaves. And then Brer Rabbit sat back on his branch and began to laugh loudly. My, how he laughed!

'Ho ho ho!' he roared. 'Ha ha ha! What a funny sight! Ha ha ha!'

Brer Bear heard the laughter, and he stopped in surprise. He looked in front of him. He looked behind him. He looked each side of him. But he couldn't see anyone laughing at all. Still the sound went on and on.

'Ho ho ho ho! Ha ha ha ha!'

Then Brer Bear looked up, and he saw old Brer Rabbit sitting on the branch laughing so much that he could hardly hold on. Every now and again Brer Rabbit would look through the leaves as if he were watching something, and then he would lean back, open his mouth and laugh.

Brer Bear watched him. He felt very curious to know what Brer Rabbit was laughing at. It must be something he was peeping at through the leaves.

At last Brer Bear could stand it no longer. He called up to Brer Rabbit, 'Heyo, Brer Rabbit! What's the matter up there? What's the joke?'

At first Brer Rabbit took no notice of Brer Bear at all, but just went on peeping through the leaves and roaring with laughter.

Brer Bear got angry and shouted at him, 'Brer Rabbit! What's the joke? What are you laughing at?'

Brer Rabbit looked down at Brer Bear. 'Heyo, Brer Bear!' he said. 'Go away, please. I'm just enjoying myself up here.'

'I can see you are,' said Brer Bear crossly. 'But please tell me the joke.'

'Well, Brer Bear, from here I can see old Mr Benjamin Ram playing his fiddle,' said Brer Rabbit, quite untruthfully. 'And he's teaching old Mrs Benjamin Ram to dance, and his two children too – and you can't imagine how funny they all look, treading on one another's toes!'

Brer Bear wanted to see them too. So he tried to climb the tree, but it was too high even for him.

'If you want to come up and see, you must get a ladder, Brer Bear,' said Brer Rabbit. 'Hurry up, now, because maybe the dancing-class will soon be over!'

Brer Bear lumbered away to his house which was nearby and fetched a ladder. He put it against the tree and climbed up to Brer Rabbit's branch.

'Now where's this funny dancing-class?' he said, and peered through the leaves. 'I can't see a thing yet.'

'Come in my place,' said Brer Rabbit, spying old Brer Fox coming along in the distance with an axe. 'I'll slip down the ladder and give you room, Brer Bear.'

So Brer Rabbit slid off the branch and gave Brer Bear his place. He slipped down that ladder at top speed, put it on his shoulder, and was away through the bushes before old Brer Fox came along with his axe.

Brer Bear sat up in the tree, grumbling away because he couldn't see Mr Benjamin Ram teaching his family to dance. Brer Fox came up, set his axe to the tree-trunk, and began to chop.

Brer Bear heard the noise and looked down.

'Hey, Brer Fox! What are you doing down there?' he called in alarm.

Brer Fox looked up in surprise. He couldn't believe his eyes when he saw Brer Bear up there instead of Brer Rabbit.

'Tails and whiskers!' he cried. 'I leave Brer Rabbit on that branch and I come back and find Brer Bear. What are *you* doing up there?'

'I'm trying to see Mr Benjamin Ram giving his family a dancing-lesson,' said Brer Bear. 'I'm told it's a mighty funny sight.'

'But how did you get up the tree?' asked Brer Fox, still surprised.

'Up the ladder, of course, silly,' said Brer Bear, thinking that Brer Fox was quite mad. He didn't know that Brer Rabbit had gone, and had taken the ladder with him.

'What ladder?' asked Brer Fox, thinking in his turn that Brer Bear was also quite mad.

'*My* ladder!' roared Brer Bear. 'Can't you see it?'

'No,' said Brer Fox. 'Where's Brer Rabbit, Brer Bear? Is he up there with you?'

'He was, just now,' said Brer Bear, looking around him in the tree. 'Maybe he's slipped down the ladder.'

Brer Fox gave a shout of anger. 'That's just what he *has* done, Brer Bear – *and* taken the

ladder with him too! What did you want to go and bring a ladder for, just when I'd got Brer Rabbit nicely caught up in the tree?'

Brer Bear stared in surprise. 'How was *I* to know that you'd got him caught?' he asked. 'When I came along, old Brer Rabbit was laughing fit to kill himself, because he said he could see Mr Benjamin Ram teaching his family to dance. So I got a ladder and came up to see too. But I haven't seen a thing yet.'

'No, and you never will,' said Brer Fox, putting his axe on his shoulder. 'But you can stay there all day and look, if you like, you silly, stupid, brainless creature!'

'Hie! Don't you say things like that to me!' said Brer Bear in a rage. 'And just you fetch me a ladder, Brer Fox, for I can't get down here without one. I'm not going to stay here all day looking at something that isn't there.'

'Oh, but you'll have to,' said Brer Fox spitefully. And he was right. Brer Bear did have to. He couldn't get down till Mrs Bear brought him another ladder that evening. As for Brer Rabbit, he laughed till the tears ran down his whiskers, whenever he thought of old Brer Fox and Brer Bear.

Brer Rabbit's bag

Now one day when Brer Rabbit was going home from market with his bag full of fish, lettuces, carrots, and meat, he met Brer Fox. Brer Fox was waiting for him behind a tree, and he jumped at Brer Rabbit as soon as he saw him.

But Brer Rabbit jumped too – and he was behind a tree before Brer Fox could say 'Got you!'

He had to drop his bag though – and Brer Fox picked it up.

'What's in here, Brer Rabbit?' he asked.

'Meat, fish, lettuces, and carrots,' said Brer Rabbit sadly.

'Well, I don't want them,' said Brer Fox. 'You can have them, if you come and get them.'

He looked quite kind, standing there, holding out the bag. Brer Rabbit thought he would see if he could grab it. So up he ran, put out his paw – but before he could snatch the bag, Brer Fox snatched *him*! And there was old Brer

Rabbit, caught in Brer Fox's paw, and shaken like a rat.

'Ha! Now you're properly caught!' said Brer Fox. 'And you'll just come along with me!'

So he dragged poor Brer Rabbit along with him, and his bag too, till he came to Brer Wolf's house. He went inside, shut the door, and showed Brer Wolf what he had caught.

'So you've got him at last!' said Brer Wolf, pleased. 'Good! Put him in that cupboard, Brer Fox, for a minute, while we get the pot a-boiling. He's so smart I believe he'd get away if we didn't lock him up!'

So Brer Rabbit was put into a cupboard, where Brer Wolf kept his brooms and pots and pans and dishes. Bang! The door was shut and locked.

Brer Rabbit sat up and shivered. This was very bad. How in the world could he get away from that cupboard before Brer Fox came back?

It was no use hiding in any of the pots and pans. He would be found. And then an idea came into old Brer Rabbit's furry head.

He took all the goods out of the bag. He put the meat into a dish on the top shelf. He put the fish into another pot. He put the lettuces and carrots into a big pan on the top shelf too. He

made a great noise doing it, and Brer Fox and Brer Wolf laughed.

'It's no good you rattling the pots and pans!' cried Brer Wolf. 'You're in there and you can't get out, Brer Rabbit!'

What did Brer Rabbit do after he had hidden his goods, but get into the bag himself and shut it – snap! There he lay, as quiet as a mouse, waiting for the door to open.

When the pot was boiling on the fire, Brer Wolf went to the door of the cupboard. He opened it very carefully, in case Brer Rabbit should rush out. But no Brer Rabbit came. He opened the door wide – where *was* Brer Rabbit?

'Hie, Brer Fox! Where's Brer Rabbit?' said Brer Wolf, peering along the shelves.

Brer Fox came up and looked. He saw the bag at the bottom of the cupboard and he threw it out into the kitchen, thinking that maybe Brer Rabbit might be hiding behind it. But no Brer Rabbit was there!

Then those two began a wild hunt for old Brer Rabbit. They hunted on every shelf – but there was no Brer Rabbit to be seen!

If only they had looked behind them they would have seen Brer Rabbit all right. He opened the bag – snap! He put out his long-eared head. He leapt out, ran to the door, opened it and disappeared under a bush. The door banged shut.

Brer Wolf and Brer Fox looked round at once. They saw the open, empty bag – and they knew at once what had happened.

'He threw out his goods, and got into the bag himself!' groaned Brer Wolf. 'Come on – after him!'

They rushed out of the house, up the path, and through the gate.

'He's gone that way, to the woods, I guess!' cried Brer Fox – and off they went to the wood. As soon as they had gone out of sight, Brer Rabbit hopped out from the bush, went into Brer Wolf's house, collected all his goods from the cupboard, slipped them once more into his bag, and, whistling merrily, skipped out of the house and away to the fields, where he knew of a good safe burrow that ran nearby his house.

And didn't he laugh loudly whenever Brer Fox and Brer Wolf came by! They went about looking as cross as two sticks for a whole month afterwards!

Brer Bear's party

ONCE Brer Bear, Brer Wolf, and Brer Fox got together, and said they'd have a party, and ask Brer Rabbit too.

'You see, Brer Bear, you don't need to get any dinner ready for us if you ask old Brer Rabbit,' grinned Brer Fox. 'All you'll want will be three plates, three knives and forks, and one good big pot of boiling water ready on the fire!'

'All right,' said Brer Bear. 'I don't feel very friendly towards Brer Rabbit just now. He's always making fun of me and tricking me. I'm just about tired of him.'

'Now don't you tell him that you've asked me and Brer Wolf,' said Brer Fox. 'Just ask him in to dinner tomorrow, and tell him you've got something special for him. Say you've got hot chestnut-pie. He loves chestnuts.'

'You leave it to me. I'll manage Brer Rabbit all right!' said Brer Bear. So he went out to find old Brer Rabbit.

He came to Brer Rabbit's house and knocked on the door, blim-blam, blim-blam!

'Who's there?' asked Brer Rabbit.

'A good friend of yours!' shouted back Brer Bear.

'Good friends ask people out to dinner!' yelled back Brer Rabbit.

'Well, that's just what I've come to ask you!' said Brer Bear. 'You come along to dinner with me tomorrow, Brer Rabbit, and I'll have a nice hot chestnut-pie for you!'

Brer Rabbit was astonished to hear such a thing from Brer Bear. He poked his head out of the window and stared at him hard. Brer Bear stared back, and didn't blink an eyelid.

'All right, I'll be along,' said Brer Rabbit, and popped his head in again.

Now the more Brer Rabbit thought about Brer Bear, the funnier he thought it was that Brer Bear should ask him to dinner.

'But I'll go,' said Brer Rabbit to himself. 'Oh yes, I'll go – and I'll come back too, though maybe Brer Bear isn't expecting me to!'

Twelve o'clock was Brer Bear's dinner-time. Brer Rabbit scuttled along to his house at half-past eleven, just to see what he could see. All he saw from outside was a mighty lot of smoke coming from Brer Bear's chimney.

'That's a mighty big fire to cook a small chestnut-pie!' said Brer Rabbit, rubbing his chin. I'll just look in at the window and see what I can see.'

So he peeped in, and all he saw was an enormous pot boiling on a big fire, and, on the table, three plates and three knives and forks. Nothing else at all.

'Funny!' said Brer Rabbit. '*Three* plates! I don't like it. No, I don't like it.'

He couldn't see anyone in the room at all. Brer Wolf and Brer Fox were hidden behind a curtain, and Brer Bear was waiting by the door.

'Shall I go and knock at the door or not?' wondered Brer Rabbit. 'Yes – I'll go – but Brer Bear won't get me indoors. No – I'll take him for a walk that he won't like!'

So Brer Rabbit marched round to the door and knocked loudly on it – BLAM, BLAM, BLAM!

Brer Bear opened it at once, and grinned all over his big mouth.

'Come along in,' he said. 'The pie is cooking.'

'Well, Brer Bear, I hope you've got shrimp sauce with it,' said Brer Rabbit, not going

indoors. 'I surely hope you have. You know, chestnut-pie is nothing without shrimp sauce.'

'Well, no I haven't got shrimp sauce,' said Brer Bear. 'But you come along in and taste the pie, Brer Rabbit. You won't want shrimp sauce, I know you won't.'

'Oh yes, I shall,' said Brer Rabbit. 'And what's more, I'm not going to eat the pie without shrimp sauce, Brer Bear. If only I'd known you'd got no shrimp sauce I'd have brought you along a whole heap of shrimps myself. There's plenty in the old well not far from here.'

'I thought shrimps were only found in the sea,' said Brer Bear, astonished.

'Not the sort of shrimps *I'm* talking about!' said Brer Rabbit.

'Well, never mind about shrimps,' said Brer Bear, hearing an impatient noise from behind the curtains. 'You come in and smell the pie, Brer Rabbit. If you don't like it, you can go.'

'I tell you I'm not going to eat any pie without hot shrimp sauce,' said Brer Rabbit. 'I'll tell you what, Brer Bear! You get your net and come along with me to the well and fish up a few shrimps. I can't reach down, I'm too short, but you could easily reach with a net.'

'Oh, all right, all right!' said Brer Bear. He went indoors and found his net.

A loud whisper came from behind the curtains, 'Don't you let Brer Rabbit out of your sight, Brer Bear! Get the shrimps and bring him back at once.'

'All right, all right,' said Brer Bear, who was beginning to feel that he was doing all the work. He went out of the house and slammed the door. Then he and Brer Rabbit set off together.

'You see, Brer Bear, nobody who is anybody ever dreams of eating chestnut-pie without shrimp sauce,' said Brer Rabbit as they went along. 'I'm really surprised that you didn't think of it.'

'Oh, you are, are you,' said Brer Bear, feeling more and more annoyed. 'Well, we'll get the silly shrimps and make them into sauce – though I guess you've got enough sauce of your own without bothering about any extra, Brer Rabbit!'

They came to the well. Brer Bear looked down into the deep, dark water. He couldn't see a single shrimp, and this was not really surprising, because there wasn't one to see!

'Ah, look! There goes a shrimp – and another – and another!' said Brer Rabbit in an

excited voice. 'Oooh, look at that fat fellow. Isn't he a lovely red colour!'

'I thought shrimps didn't go red till they were cooked,' said Brer Bear, surprised.

'These shrimps are not like the ones you've seen before,' said Brer Rabbit firmly. 'Quick, Brer Bear – catch them, catch them! Put in your net!'

Brer Bear put in his net, hoping that a few shrimps would swim into it, for he couldn't see a single one to catch. But his net wouldn't quite reach.

'Lean right over, lean right over!' cried Brer Rabbit. 'Then your net will reach!'

'Well, hold on to my trousers then,' said Brer Bear.

So Brer Rabbit caught hold of the seat of Brer Bear's trousers, and Brer Bear leaned right over to make his net reach the water.

And then suddenly Brer Rabbit let go Brer Bear's trousers – and down he went into the well, splish, splash!

'Oooble, oooble, ooble,' gurgled poor Brer Bear, spluttering and choking as he came up again, and floundered about in the water. 'Brer Rabbit, you let me go! And just look here – there isn't a single shrimp to be seen! They're not real!'

'They're just as real as your chestnut-pie, Brer Bear!' grinned Brer Rabbit, leaning over the top of the well. 'Yes, just as real! Good-bye! I hope you enjoy your bathe!'

He skipped off back to Brer Bear's house, dancing as he went. He poked his head in at the door and yelled to Brer Wolf and Brer Fox, 'Heyo, there! Brer Bear says there are such a lot of shrimps down that well, he wants some help. Hurry along, hurry along!'

Brer Fox and Brer Wolf rushed to the well to get some of the shrimps, but all they saw there was a very wet, very cold, and very angry bear!

'Get him out and give him some of that hot chestnut-pie!' yelled Brer Rabbit, dancing about in the distance. 'He can have my share – and tell him he can have sauce from Brer Rabbit, instead of from shrimps! He'll like that, he will!'

And off went Brer Rabbit in delight, stopping every now and again to roll on the ground and laugh like twenty hyenas!

Brer Rabbit and the tongs

ONCE Brer Rabbit went to get a present for his old wife. She wanted a pair of tongs for the fire, and a nice poker.

'And see you get a *long* poker and a *long* pair of tongs!' she said. 'The fire gets so hot sometimes that I can't get near it to put another log on the fire. A long pair of tongs will save my whiskers getting singed off!'

So Brer Rabbit went to town and he bought a fine long pair of tongs and a fine long poker. He put the poker under his arm, and hung the tongs round his neck. Then back he went through the woods, whistling like a blackbird.

Old Brer Fox heard the whistling and he knew who it was. He shot along to meet Brer Rabbit, and waited for him behind a tree. He heard him coming along merrily, and he grinned to himself to think what a shock he was going to give Brer Rabbit.

When Brer Rabbit came up to the tree, Brer

Fox rushed out like a whirlwind. He pounced on Brer Rabbit and held him fast.

'Now, let go, let go!' cried old Brer Rabbit in a fright. But Brer Fox didn't mean to let go! He held Brer Rabbit tightly, and gave him a shake.

The tongs and the poker banged together and made a clanking noise.

'What are those?' asked Brer Fox in astonishment. He had never seen fire-irons before, and he couldn't imagine what they were.

'Brer Fox, if you let me go, I'll give you these wonderful, marvellous things,' said Brer Rabbit at once.

'Why, what do they do?' asked Brer Fox.

'Well, you see this?' said Brer Rabbit, taking the tongs from round his neck, and opening and shutting them. 'Now you've only got to say what you want to eat, and you'll see it appear between these tongs, they'll hold it for you – like that.

Brer Rabbit let the tongs shut with a clang.

'And what's the other thing for?' asked Brer Fox, looking at the long steel poker.

'I'll show you what that's for, when you've seen what the tongs can do,' said Brer Rabbit. 'Now, Brer Fox, you just let me go, and you can have these marvellous things.'

'I'll not let you go till you show me what they do,' said Brer Fox firmly. 'I've had enough of your tricks, Brer Rabbit. I'm just going to hold on to you till you show me what all these things can do.'

'All right, all right,' said Brer Rabbit. 'I'll show you. Let me open these tongs again – and point them at you – like that. Now, you must shut your eyes and wish for what you want – and maybe when you open them again you'll get a fine surprise!'

'I shall still keep hold of you!' said Brer Fox, and he held Brer Rabbit fast by the sleeve. He shut his eyes and thought of roast duck. If only he could see a roast duck between those tongs when he opened his eyes! 'Brer Rabbit said I should get a surprise!' he thought.

He did get a surprise – but it wasn't the surprise he wanted! No – it was a most unpleasant surprise. He suddenly felt something biting his nose hard – squeezing it, pinching it! He let Brer Rabbit go and put his paws up to his poor nose at once, howling and yelling!

He opened his eyes, and saw that the tongs had got hold of his nose. Brer Rabbit was pinching his nose with them as hard as he could. The tongs

were so long that once Brer Fox let go Brer Rabbit's sleeve, Brer Rabbit could stand far enough away not to be caught again.

Brer Fox tried to get the tongs off his nose. He tried to grab Brer Rabbit. He howled with rage. He danced about in pain. But Brer Rabbit wouldn't let go!

'Loose me! Loose me!' cried Brer Fox, trying to push the tongs off his nose. 'Let me go, let me go!'

'You wanted to know what the tongs were for,' said Brer Rabbit, 'and now I'm showing you! And you wanted to know what the poker was for, and I'll show you that too!"

And with that Brer Rabbit began to poke poor Brer Fox in the ribs till he howled with rage. Poke, poke, poke!

'Ow, ow, ow!'

Poke, poke, poke!

'Ow, ow, ow!'

'Now get along, please,' said Brer Rabbit, still holding Brer Fox with the tongs, and poking him with the poker. 'Get along! I've got to get home to dinner, and I'm not staying here all day!'

So poor Brer Fox had to walk backwards, with Brer Rabbit grabbing his long nose with the tongs, and poking him with the poker. When Brer Rabbit got up his front path, he yelled to his wife to open the door.

As soon as it was open, he opened the tongs, let go Brer Fox's nose, slipped inside the door, and bolted it! He looked out of the window.

'So glad you know how to use tongs and poker now!' he called. 'Come and call on me again if you ever want another lesson.'

Brer Fox didn't answer. He ran off, with his nose in his paws, and asked Brer Bear to bandage it for him. Brer Bear roared with laughter to see him with a bandage round his nose.

'You can't talk and you can't eat!' he said. 'You'd better keep out of old Brer Rabbit's way for the next few days, Brer Fox, or he'll kill himself with laughing at you!'

So Brer Fox vanished for a week and nursed his nose. Poor old Brer Fox, he just *can't* get the better of Brer Rabbit!

Brer Wolf gets a surprise

ONCE, when Brer Rabbit was gambolling through the wood, singing a silly little song that he had made up, he heard a curious noise.

He stopped his song and listened. He didn't hear the noise again, so he went on singing:

Oh, if I were a little bee,
Humming round a jim-jam tree,
It would be curious to see
Growing on the end of me
Not a tail or anything
Except a most unpleasant sting!
Zz, zz, zz, zz . . .

Brer Rabbit stopped his song suddenly again, because he had heard the peculiar noise. He stood and listened, and didn't sing again. The noise seemed to come from a tree nearby.

Brer Rabbit looked up into the tree. Nothing there. He walked all round the tree and back again. Nothing there!

But still the noise went on, 'Hissssss! Spit! Hissssss! Yee-ow, ee-ow! Hisssssssssss!'

'Funny!' said Brer Rabbit, staring up into the tree again. 'Nobody there – and yet it sounds like a houseful of cats in a temper!'

Brer Rabbit climbed up the tree a little way – and then he came to a hole. He peered down into the hole. At once a great noise came from the hole that startled Brer Rabbit so much he nearly fell down the tree.

'Baby wild-cats!' said Brer Rabbit. 'Yes, that's what's making all the noise. Poor little things – their mother has gone off and left them. I guess I'd better take them home with me and give them some milk.'

Brer Rabbit fetched his bag, which he had left on the ground. Then he took out his silk handkerchief and let it down into the hole. One of the kittens hissed and spat at it, and then dug its claws into the silk. Brer Rabbit quickly lifted up his handkerchief, kitten and all! He dropped the kitten into the bag, shook the hanky free from its claws, and put it down to catch the next kitten. Up it came, clawing at the handkerchief, and was dropped into the bag.

There were five kittens altogether, all as wild

and fierce as each other. What a noise they made! How they fought inside the bag! How they yowled and scratched at one another! Really, it was terrible to hear them.

'Fight all you like!' said Brer Rabbit, putting the bag over his shoulders. 'I know it's what you wild kittens like better than anything! Fight all you like!'

Now as he went along home, with his bag of kittens on his shoulder, who should come pounding along through the wood but old Brer Wolf, looking mighty hungry and mighty fierce. He saw Brer Rabbit and pounced on him before Brer Rabbit could slip round the trees.

'Ha!' said Brer Wolf, and his whiskers shot up and down. 'Ha! So you're home from market, are you, with your bag full of goodies. Well, you just hand it over to *me*!'

'Let me go, Brer Wolf,' said Brer Rabbit, wriggling. 'Your claws are sharp. And don't you be silly enough to take my bag either!'

'What's in the bag?' asked Brer Wolf, sniffing.

'A litter of wild kittens,' said Brer Rabbit. 'And my, they're wild, I can tell you!'

Brer Wolf laughed loudly. 'Do you suppose I'm going to believe that you are carrying a bag of wild kittens about with you, Brer Rabbit?' he asked. 'No – I guess that bag's full of good meat!'

The kittens had all become perfectly quiet when they heard Brer Wolf's voice, for they were afraid of him. So they didn't say a word. They just lay as quiet as could be in the bag.

'You give that bag to me, Brer Rabbit,' said Brer Wolf. 'If you don't, I'll take it –and you too!'

Now just at that moment Brer Rabbit caught sight of two bright green eyes gleaming through the trees – and he saw that it was the mother wild-cat! She hadn't really left her kittens – she had just gone to get a drink of water from the stream for herself. When she had gone back she had found her tree-hole empty, and she had flown into a tremendous rage.

She called her mate, and he called five other wild-cats.

'We will go to find the stolen kittens!' hissed Cousin Wild-cat. 'Follow me!'

And that was how it was that Brer Rabbit suddenly saw the fierce and angry eyes of the mother wild-cat, and, behind her, six more pairs of green eyes too! He began to shiver and shake, for an army of wild-cats is the fiercest thing in the world!

'All right,' he said to Brer Wolf. 'You take my bag of meat. Here you are, you're welcome to it!'

He pushed his bag into Brer Wolf's arms and then slipped behind a tree. Brer Wolf was pleased.

'Ho!' he shouted after Brer Rabbit. 'You're a little coward, you are! You'd run away from anything!'

He opened the bag, meaning to eat the meat at once – and out sprang five wild kittens, all their claws out, spitting and hissing and snarling like a hundred fireworks going off together!

Brer Wolf got a dreadful shock – but an even bigger one was waiting for him.

As soon as the seven wild-cats saw their kittens jumping out of the bag, they gave a snarl and leapt on poor, scared Brer Wolf!

My word, they were like a swarm of big bees all over him! He shook them off and they came again. Their claws dug into him like hundreds of pins and needles, and they spat and hissed like kettles on the boil!

'We'll teach you. Hisssssssss!'

'We'll teach you to take our kittens!' snarled cousin Wild-cat.

Brer Wolf shook the cats off his big brown

hairy body and ran for his life. The wild-cats picked up the delighted kittens and ran back to the hollow tree with them, meowling in joy.

Brer Rabbit popped his head out of a hole as Brer Wolf rushed by, scratched and torn.

'Hallo, Brer Wolf!' he cried. 'My, how dreadful you look! Have you been shot out of a gun or something?'

'Now look here, Brer Rabbit, if I'd known that bag was full of wild kittens, I'd have run a mile!' said Brer Wolf angrily.

'What a little coward you are, Brer Wolf!' said Brer Rabbit. 'You'd run away from anything! I *told* you the bag was full of kittens!'

'Grrrrrrrrrr!' said Brer Wolf, and tore home to bandage all his scratches. He did look a funny sight when he had finished!

Brer Rabbit is very kind

ONCE Brer Bear got very tired of Brer Rabbit, and he made up his mind to get him, if it took him a month of Sundays to do it.

'I'll just go round and follow him everywhere,' thought Brer Bear to himself. 'Sooner or later I'll surprise him and get him all right. Then that will be the end of his tricks.'

So Brer Bear began to follow Brer Rabbit around all day and every day. Brer Rabbit thought it was funny at first, and he took Brer Bear a lot of long walks till Brer Bear was tired out.

But Brer Rabbit was tired out too, so he soon gave that up. He got very angry with Brer Bear. If he went into his garden, there was Brer Bear standing by the gate. If he went to walk in the woods, Brer Bear was sure to be hiding behind a tree. If he went to get water from the well, Brer Bear would be sitting the other side, waiting to catch him.

'This is making me feel scared,' said Brer Rabbit to himself at last. 'I can't keep looking out for Brer Bear every minute of the day and night. Maybe he'll give up. He'll get tired of it.'

But once Brer Bear had made up his mind to anything, there was no stopping him, and no tiring him. He just went on and on and on. It was most annoying.

And then Brer Rabbit began to think. He sat down and he thought and thought how he might make things better for himself. Then he jumped up, slapped his knee, and capered off to town to buy something.

Brer Bear lumbered after him, but Brer Rabbit got there a long way first. He went to a shop that sold watches and he asked to see some. He put each watch to his ear and listened to it.

'I want the one with the very loudest tick,' he said.

'Well, most people want a quiet watch,' said the shopman. 'But I've got an old watch that has a tick like a grandfather clock! Maybe that would suit you!'

He brought out a big old watch whose tick was certainly very loud indeed! Brer Rabbit was pleased. He bought the watch and then set off to the post office with it. He posted it to Brer Bear with a note inside.

The note said:

'DEAR BRER BEAR, – I'm mighty glad you are following Brer Rabbit about. Here's a reward for your patience. Please wear it, with best wishes from

COUSIN WILD-CAT.'

Brer Bear was surprised and delighted with the letter and the watch.

'Dear me,' he said, putting the watch into his pocket, 'I'd no idea Cousin Wild-cat knew what I was doing. What a generous creature he is! I'll ask him to dinner when I've got Brer Rabbit at last.'

And now Brer Rabbit didn't need to keep a look-out for Brer Bear everywhere, because as soon as he came anywhere near him, he always heard the same warning sound:

'TICK, TOCK, TICK, TOCK!'

Then Brer Rabbit would shout out loudly, 'Heyo, Brer Bear! I can see you! Peep-bo!'

And Brer Bear would be most astonished, if he was hiding right inside a bush or down a hole. It didn't seem to matter where he hid, Brer Rabbit always seemed to see him and shout loudly, 'Heyo, Brer Bear! I can see you! Peep-bo!'

Brer Bear hid up a tree, and the leaves were thick around him. But as soon as Brer Rabbit came along that way he pricked up his ears and heard 'TICK, TOCK, TICK, TOCK!' from Brer Bear's big new watch. Then he would stop and cry, 'Peep-bo! Peep-bo! I can see you, Brer Bear! It's no good trying to hide from *me!*'

Brer Bear once hid himself under a great rock, and he knew Brer Rabbit couldn't possibly see him. But that wasn't a bit of good either, for as soon as Brer Rabbit came pattering by, he stopped and shouted, 'Oh, so you're there, are you, Brer Bear! Playing peep-bo again! What a funny fellow you are!'

Brer Bear gave it up after a week or two, and Brer Fox asked him why.

'Oh, Brer Rabbit has got eyes like a hundred eagles!' said Brer Bear in disgust. 'He can see through trees and walls and rocks! It's just no good at all, Brer Fox.'

'Well, let me hide the other side of this thick wall with you, Brer Bear,' said Brer Fox. 'I guess he can't really see through that!'

So the two of them sat down and hid – and presently along came Brer Rabbit, lippitty, clippitty, lippitty, clippitty, as usual. And he heard the sound of Brer Bear's watch again, 'TICK, TOCK, TICK, TOCK, TICK, TOCK!'

He saw the print of Brer Fox's feet too, and he grinned.

'So Brer Fox is there too!' he said to himself. 'Well, he won't be there long!'

He went to the nearby well and filled the bucket with water. He carried it to the wall – and, slishy-slosh, all the water poured down on to the heads of the alarmed Brer Bear and Brer Fox!

'Peep-bo, Brer Bear! Peep-bo, Brer Fox!' cried Brer Rabbit, standing on the top of the wall. 'Did you think I couldn't see through the

wall? Oh yes, I can – and I saw you both sitting there, as snug as can be! This is a fine game you're playing – but I shall always win it!'

Brer Fox sprang away and Brer Bear lumbered after him.

'What's the good of hiding and waiting for a person that has got eyes like that?' grumbled Brer Bear.

'No good at all!' said Brer Fox, and he shook the water from his coat. 'Just leave him alone, Brer Bear. That's the best thing to do with Brer Rabbit.'

And you may be sure that Brer Rabbit quite agreed!

Brer Rabbit and the big wind

ONCE when Brer Rabbit was out walking, the wind got up and the trees began to sway. Brer Rabbit liked the wind. He held out his coat, let the wind fill it like a sail, and then off he went at top speed through the woods, shouting for joy.

Now Brer Bear was coming along, and suddenly Brer Rabbit bumped into him, and knocked all the breath out of his body. Brer Bear clutched at Brer Rabbit and held on tight.

'What's the matter now? What's all this? Why are you running so fast?' growled old Brer Bear angrily. 'Knocking a fellow down like this – what's scaring you, Brer Rabbit?'

Brer Rabbit didn't like being held so tightly by Brer Bear. He wriggled and struggled, and he shouted in Brer Bear's ear.

'It's the big wind! My, I was running away from the big wind. And you'd better run too, I guess, Brer Bear, because if the big wind can blow a little fellow like me along so fast, what will it do to a big man like you? My, it will take you through the wood and drop you into the river as easy as can be!'

'Stars and moon!' said Brer Bear, frightened. 'Where shall I hide?'

'Down a hole, Brer Bear, down a hole!' cried Brer Rabbit. 'Quick, find a big one and get down it!'

Brer Bear let Brer Rabbit go and then lumbered off to a hole he knew. He squeezed down it, backwards way, and lay there with his head at the opening.

'The wind will blow your head off, Brer Bear!' cried Brer Rabbit, enjoying himself.

'Oh, what shall I do with it?' groaned Brer Bear.

'I'll put a big stone in front of the hole,' said Brer Rabbit. 'Then you'll be safe.'

So he rolled a great stone in front of the hole, and then giggled to think how nicely he had trapped Brer Bear.

But he didn't grin long. No – he turned round, and there was old Brer Fox, ready to pounce on him! Brer Rabbit gave a squeal and stepped backwards.

'Now, you leave me alone!' he shouted to Brer

Fox. 'If you don't, I'll teach you such a lesson!'

'You speak boldly, Brer Rabbit,' said Brer Fox, and he reached out his paw. 'You won't speak quite so boldly in a minute.'

'Now you listen to me, Brer Fox!' cried Brer Rabbit, squeezing into a bush as far as he could. 'You just listen to me! If you so much as touch me I'll do the same to you as I've just done to Brer Bear!'

'And what's that?' asked Brer Fox, still grinning.

'I'll squash you down a hole and put a big stone in front of you,' said Brer Rabbit.

Brer Fox laughed and laughed. 'You show me where you've squashed Brer Bear into a hole, and I'll believe you,' he said.

'Come along then,' said Brer Rabbit, and he led Brer Fox round the bush to the hole where Brer Bear lay. Brer Bear was moaning and groaning because he felt very tightly squeezed in the hole – but he couldn't get out because of the big stone in front.

'There you are!' said Brer Rabbit. 'Can't you hear him? Heyo, Brer Bear! Just tell old Brer Fox here that I rolled this stone in front of the hole. He won't believe me.'

'Well, it's true enough,' said Brer Bear with a groan, trying to get more comfortable. 'Yes, Brer Rabbit put the stone there all right, Brer Fox. Oh, Brer Rabbit, let me out again now! I'm mighty uncomfortable.'

Well, of course, Brer Fox didn't know that Brer Bear had gone into the hole because he was afraid of the big wind – he just thought Brer Rabbit had squashed him into it himself, and had kept him there with the big stone.

So he looked mighty queer, and edged away from Brer Rabbit, feeling scared. Brer Rabbit grinned.

'Well,' he said, 'do you want to try and catch me now, Brer Fox? You're welcome! But I warn you, I'll put you into a hole too, and keep you there with a big stone in front till you say you're sorry. I think I'll put you there anyhow – yes, I will! Come here, Brer Fox, come here! I want to put you into a hole!'

But Brer Fox wasn't stopping. He fled away with a howl, wondering how it was that old Brer Rabbit seemed to be so strong all of a sudden.

And Brer Rabbit tore after him for all he was worth, though he didn't mean to catch him. No – not he! It was just a bit of fun chasing

somebody who wanted to chase *him* – and how all the other creatures stared when they saw Brer Fox running away from old Brer Rabbit!

As for Brer Bear, he lay in his hole all day till Brer Wolf came along and let him out. And my, wasn't he angry with Brer Rabbit! You'd better keep out of Brer Bear's way for a week or two, Brer Rabbit, or you'll be sorry.

Brer Rabbit is so clever

Now once old Brer Rabbit had a fine store of jam in the barn, that Mrs Rabbit had made. There wasn't room to put it in the larder, so Brer Rabbit made some shelves in his little barn and put the jam there.

But old Brer Bear soon sniffed it out and he went one night to take some. He got in through the window and went off with seven pots of fine strawberry jam. Brer Rabbit was so angry next day when he found the seven pots missing.

'I'll catch Brer Bear and make him pay dearly for that jam!' said Brer Rabbit to himself. So he went off to find some straw, and put it down in the barn. Then he went to the holly tree and looked under it for some sharp-pointed fallen leaves.

Brer Rabbit mixed the sharp holly leaves in with the straw, grinning away to himself all the time. Now whoever came stealing at night would tread on a prickly leaf and get a shock!

Well, that night along came old Brer Bear for a few more pots of jam again. He climbed in through the window and went to the shelf of jam – and on the way he trod heavily on a sharp-pointed holly leaf! He let out a yell and hopped round in pain.

Brer Rabbit was outside, waiting. He opened the door and rushed in with a big stick. He pretended not to know that Brer Bear was there and he slashed about in the straw as if he was mad!

'I'll get that snake!' he shouted, as he slashed about. 'I'll get that snake! It won't bite me if I know anything about it! I'll get that snake!'

Well, when Brer Bear heard Brer Rabbit shouting about a snake he got very frightened. Was it a snake that had bitten his foot? Oh my, oh my, he might be poisoned and die!

Brer Bear let out a groan and Brer Rabbit stopped slashing about and spoke as if he was mighty surprised.

'Who's there?' he asked.

'It's me – Brer Bear,' said Brer Bear, lumbering over to Brer Rabbit in the darkness. 'Oh, Brer Rabbit, I think that snake's bitten me!'

He trod on another holly leaf and let out such a yell that he made Brer Rabbit jump.

'It's bitten me again!' he shouted. 'It's bitten me again! Oh, Brer Rabbit, I'll die! I've been bitten twice by a poisonous snake in the straw.'

'Well,' said Brer Rabbit, severely, 'I should like to know what you are doing stamping about in my straw at this time of night, Brer Bear.'

'Oh, Brer Rabbit, this is no time for asking silly questions,' groaned Brer Bear, holding first one foot and then another. 'I'm bitten, I tell you. Fetch a doctor.'

'Well, first please tell me what you were doing in my barn?' said Brer Rabbit fiercely.

'Oh, Brer Rabbit, if you must know, I was after your jam,' groaned Brer Bear. 'And now, please go and get a doctor. Do you want me to die of snake-bite in your barn?'

'Well, it might serve you right,' said Brer Rabbit, grinning away to himself in the dark, thinking of the holly leaves in the straw.

Brer Bear tried to get to the door, but unluckily he trod on yet another holly leaf. He gave such a yell that the windows shook!

'That snake's bitten me again! Oh, oh, what shall I do? Go fetch a doctor quickly, Brer Rabbit! You can have back your seven pots of jam!'

'And what else?' demanded Brer Rabbit.

'Oh, you can have seven pots of honey, too,' wept Brer Bear.

'Anything else?' asked Brer Rabbit.

'Yes – you can have seven pots of tomato chutney,' groaned Brer Bear. Brer Rabbit licked his lips. Mrs Bear's tomato chutney was simply delicious!

'Well, I'll go and get it all now,' said Brer Rabbit. 'Now you stay here, Brer Bear, because if you go stamping about the barn that snake is sure to bite you again!'

Off sped Brer Rabbit. He came to Brer Bear's house and got the jam, the honey, and the chutney. He tore back again and set it neatly on the shelf. Brer Bear was lying groaning in the straw, not daring to move.

'I think my legs are swelling up,' he said feebly. 'I think I'm poisoned all over.'

'Well, I'll put some wonderful snake-ointment on you,' said Brer Rabbit, grinning away in the darkness. 'It will soon make you right!'

Brer Rabbit went into his house and got a tin of black boot-polish. He went to the barn with a lantern.

'Oh, Brer Rabbit, you are kind,' said Brer

Bear. 'Just rub the ointment on and I can go to the doctor then. Rub it on quickly.'

Brer Rabbit smeared black boot-polish all over Brer Bear's feet. It smelt horrid.

'There!' he said. 'You will find that your feet won't hurt you at all tomorrow. This is wonderful for snake-bites.'

Brer Bear cheered up and began to feel better at once. He stood up – and trod on yet another holly leaf! He sat down with a groan.

'There must be heaps of snakes here,' he said. 'Put some more ointment on, Brer Rabbit!'

So old Brer Rabbit rubbed more black boot-polish on, grinning away.

'Now, Brer Bear, just you listen to me,' he said. 'As soon as you get home, lick off all this ointment and put a fresh lot on out of the tin. Don't forget, will you? If you do that, you won't need to go to the doctor.'

'Oh, thank you, Brer Rabbit,' said Brer Bear gratefully. He hobbled out of the barn, and did not tread on any more holly leaves! Off he went home, glad to find that his legs didn't hurt him at all.

'That must be wonderful ointment Brer Rabbit gave me!' he said to himself. 'I will lick it off and put on some more as soon as I get home.'

So he sat down when he got home and began to lick off the black boot-polish. It tasted simply terrible. Brer Bear didn't know how he was going to lick it all off. He sat with his tongue hanging out, feeling mighty sick. Then he began licking again – but he just *had* to stop, for the taste was dreadful.

'I'll put the fresh ointment on top of the old,' he said at last, and picked up the tin. On it he read, 'Black boot-polish!' Brer Bear stared as if he simply couldn't believe his eyes!

'*Boot*-polish! And I've been licking it! *Boot*-polish!' shouted Brer Bear, and he went to rinse

out his mouth. But he couldn't get the black off his tongue!

And for two whole weeks, whenever Brer Rabbit met Brer Bear he shouted out, 'How's your tongue, Brer Bear? How's your tongue? Let's have a look at your tongue!'

Didn't Brer Bear growl! He'd lost seven pots of honey and seven pots of chutney – and got his tongue well blacked! Poor Brer Bear – he won't go stealing from old Brer Rabbit again!

Brer Rabbit and the glue

ONCE Brer Rabbit had a job to do in his garden. Some little bits of his fence had broken, and he guessed he would stick them back with glue.

So he put the glue-pot on the fire, stirred it up, and when it had melted he took it into the garden. He gathered together the bits of wood that wanted sticking, and began.

He was so busy that he didn't notice Brer Fox coming up behind him. It was only when Brer Fox pounced on him that he knew Brer Fox was there.

'Got you!' cried Brer Fox.

'Now Brer Fox, please let me go,' said Brer Rabbit in a calm sort of voice. 'Can't you see I'm very busy?'

'What's that matter?' said Brer Fox, still holding tightly to Brer Rabbit. 'I shall be busy soon too – having you for my dinner!'

'Oh, Brer Fox, don't be mean,' said Brer Rabbit. 'Just let me finish this job, for goodness' sake! I promised I would do it today, and I always like to keep my promises.'

'What are you doing?' asked Brer Fox, gazing round at the glue-brushes, the glue-pot, and the wood.

'I'm mending this fence with glue,' said Brer Rabbit. 'Now don't ask if you can help, Brer Fox, because you couldn't. It's too tricky a job for you.'

'What do you mean – too tricky for me?' said Brer Fox crossly. 'You're not trying to make out that you are cleverer than I am, are you?'

'Oh no, not at all,' said Brer Rabbit, dipping his brush in the glue. 'It's only that I think you would make a mess of it.'

Brer Fox glared at Brer Rabbit, who was now peacefully painting a board with strong glue. 'Look here, Brer Rabbit,' he began.

'Can't. I'm busy,' answered Brer Rabbit. 'Let me finish this job and I'll come with you, Brer Fox. But for goodness' sake don't interfere. I don't want everything spoilt.'

Of course that made Brer Fox snatch up a big glue-brush and start work at once.

'Hoo! I'll show you that I can glue things just as well as you can,' he growled.

Brer Rabbit noticed that Brer Fox's tail was brushing against the garden-gate behind them. He grinned to himself. He put down his glue-brush and picked up the piece of wood he was working on to see if it was nicely done. When he set to work again, he didn't pick up his glue-brush – no, he took Brer Fox's tail, and dipped that into the glue-pot instead!

Brer Fox was angry. 'Hey, you cuckoo! That's my tail!'

'Sorry,' said Brer Rabbit. 'It's so like a brush, Brer Fox. Sorry, sorry, sorry!'

Brer Fox took his tail out of the glue-pot and arranged it behind him again. It touched the gate as before. And pretty soon it stuck hard to the gate. Brer Rabbit watched out of the corner of his eye and grinned away to himself.

'I'll just go and get some more glue,' he said to Brer Fox after a while, and he got up. Brer Fox got up to go with him, for he wasn't going to let Brer Rabbit go out of his sight, now that he had caught him so neatly. But something held him by the tail.

Brer Fox swung round angrily – and saw that his tail was stuck fast to the gate.

GLUE

'My tail's stuck!' he cried. 'Brer Rabbit, you did it on purpose! Unstick it at once.'

'What – and let you pounce on me again!' grinned Brer Rabbit. 'I'm not such a silly as you think, Brer Fox. You can stay there all day, if you like.'

'I shall *not*!' yelled Brer Fox, and he tugged at his tail. Then he groaned deeply, for it hurt him very much. He sat and scowled at Brer Rabbit, who stood just out of reach, swinging the glue-pot.

'I'll get you a pair of scissors and you can cut your tail off,' said Brer Rabbit kindly.

'Don't be silly,' said Brer Fox, groaning again.

'There's no pleasing you,' said Brer Rabbit. 'So good-bye. I'll be back again soon to see how your tail is getting on.'

Brer Rabbit went indoors, and watched from the window. He knew Brer Wolf was coming along that way soon – and sure enough he soon came ambling by. He pushed open Brer Rabbit's gate to see if Brer Rabbit was anywhere about, and he nearly knocked over Brer Fox, who was just the other side of it, his tail still stuck tightly to the gate.

'Hie! Be careful!' yelled Brer Fox.

'Heyo, Brer Fox,' said Brer Wolf in surprise. 'What are you doing here?'

'I'm stuck,' said Brer Fox.

'Stuck? What do you mean, "stuck"?' said Brer Wolf in still greater surprise.

'Don't you know what "stuck" means?' said Brer Fox snappily. 'My tail's stuck to the gate. That tiresome Brer Rabbit did it. Now he's offered me a pair of scissors to cut off my tail.'

'Well, that's what you'll have to do, isn't it?' said Brer Wolf, looking at the stuck-fast tail. 'You'll have to stay here all night and day if you don't.'

'Now do you think I'm going to cut off my beautiful tail?' demanded Brer Fox. 'You must be mad!'

'Well, what else is there to do?' said Brer Wolf.

'I don't know,' said Brer Fox sulkily.

'Ah – *I* know!' cried Brer Wolf. 'I can take the gate off! Then you can go home, carrying the gate, can't you?'

'Well – it sounds silly, but perhaps it's the best thing to do,' said Brer Fox gloomily. 'Brer Rabbit will lose his gate then – and serve him right!'

Brer Wolf heaved at the gate till it came off its hinges. Then Brer Fox took it on his back, with

his tail still tightly stuck to it, and walked slowly off home, groaning all the way because of the weight of the gate and the pain in his tail.

When he got home he asked Brer Wolf to get a great bath of hot water. When it was ready, Brer Fox sat beside it, with his tail and the gate in the water, hoping to soak off the glue.

It came off after twelve hours' soaking, and poor Brer Fox got such a cold in his tail that he had to wear a handkerchief round it for three days to keep his tail from sneezing itself off.

He chopped up Brer Rabbit's gate and burnt it, and the next day found to his great rage that his own gate was gone – and there it was swinging gaily in Brer Rabbit's gateway.

'You just wait, Brer Rabbit, you just wait,' he yelled.

'Righto!' yelled back Brer Rabbit. 'I don't know what you want me to wait for, Brer Fox, but I'll certainly wait. Oh yes, I'll wait all right!'

So he's waiting – and Brer Fox's gate is still swinging merrily in Brer Rabbit's front garden. It *is* so annoying for Brer Fox!

Brer Rabbit saves Miss Goose

Now one day when Brer Rabbit was lying snoozing just inside a bramble bush, Brer Fox came along with Brer Bear.

It was a hot day, and Brer Bear wanted a rest. So the two of them sat down beside the bramble bush and began to talk.

Brer Rabbit didn't so much as twitch a whisker. Not he! He knew that Brer Fox could reach a paw into his bush and drag him out as easy as winking. So there he lay and tried not to breathe, in case Brer Fox and Brer Bear heard him.

Brer Fox started to talk about old Miss Goose, who was very fat.

'She keeps her door locked at night,' he said, 'but I know she opens her window in this hot weather. I'm planning to creep in, Brer Bear, and catch old Miss Goose. My, she's fat!'

'You let me help you, Brer Fox,' said Brer Bear at once. 'You could never carry Miss Goose away alone. You go in and hit her, and I'll help you to carry her away.'

'Well, we'll try tonight,' said Brer Fox. 'You wait outside the window and I'll throw her out to you. You hurry off with her whilst I tidy up the room and pull the bed together a bit. I guess she'll try to fight me and there'll be feathers all over the place.'

Brer Rabbit lay still in the bush and listened to all this. He liked old Miss Goose, and he was angry to hear what Brer Fox planned. As soon as Brer Fox and Brer Bear had gone, he sprang to his feet and ran to his house.

He looked through all his cupboards and drawers to find something he wanted. It was a tiny green thing, made of rubber. Brer Rabbit grinned and put it into his pocket. Then he set off for old Miss Goose's house.

She was hanging up some washing on the line.

'Good-day, Miss Goose,' said Brer Rabbit. 'I've bad news for you. Brer Fox and Brer Bear are going to come and catch you tonight.'

'Oh lawks! Oh lawks!' cackled Miss Goose, in a dreadful flurry at once. 'What am I to do, what am I to do? I'd get Mr Dog to come and protect me, but he's gone to see his uncle.'

'Now don't you get in such a way about it,' said Brer Rabbit. 'Just you go and spend the night with your cousin, Miss Feathers, and I'll see that Brer Fox and Brer Bear get such a fright they'll never come near you again!'

'Oh, Brer Rabbit, that's mighty kind of you,' said Miss Goose, shaking out her feathers and looking very fat. 'I'll pack my bag now and rush off this minute! Oh, the wicked creatures! Mind you give them a scare, Brer Rabbit.'

'I'll do that!' said Brer Rabbit with a grin. He took the little green rubber thing out of his pocket and showed it to Miss Goose.

'This is an air-balloon,' he said. 'I had it at Christmas-time. When it blows up, it takes the shape of a big bird. I'll blow it up as big as it will go, and then I'll take one of your night-dresses, Miss Goose, and dress the bird-balloon up in it. I'll put it into your bed tonight, and maybe I'll have some fun when Brer Fox comes along.'

'Well, I'll be right back tomorrow,' said Miss Goose. She stuffed some things into her old bag and set off down the hill, waddling in a great hurry. Wicked Brer Fox! Wicked Brer Bear! She hoped Brer Rabbit would punish them properly.

Brer Rabbit blew up the balloon. He blew it up mighty carefully, for he didn't want it to burst. When it was almost as big as Miss Goose, he tied up the end tightly. Then he took one of Miss Goose's enormous white night-dresses and dressed the balloon in it. He laughed and laughed, for it was the funniest sight in the world to see a balloon wobbling about the room in one of Miss Goose's white nighties.

Brer Rabbit tied a string to the waist of the night-dress, and then waited for the night to come. He locked the door and opened the window a little as Miss Goose always did.

He left the balloon-goose standing in the middle of the floor. He went under the bed with the string. Pretty soon he heard the sound of whispering outside, and he pricked up his ears. He saw Brer Fox's head as Brer Fox peeped in at the window. Then he heard him whisper again.

'Miss Goose is just going to bed,' whispered Brer Fox to Brer Bear. 'She's standing on the floor in her white night-dress. My, she's fat!'

Brer Rabbit pulled the string he held and the balloon-goose bobbed up and down a bit and seemed to walk here and there. Brer Rabbit had to stuff his paw into his mouth to keep from laughing, for the balloon-goose looked the funniest creature in the world.

'She's walking about the bedroom!' whispered Brer Fox to Brer Bear. 'She's just ready to get into bed.'

Brer Rabbit pulled the string and the balloon-goose wobbled towards the bed. Brer Rabbit waited till Brer Fox had bobbed down again and then he quickly popped the balloon-goose into the bed, and pulled the clothes over it.

Brer Fox peeped again.

'She's got into bed,' he whispered. 'My, what a hill she makes under the bed-clothes! It's a good thing you came to help me carry her, Brer Bear!'

Brer Fox crept in at the window. He tiptoed to the bed. He had his stick in his hand, and he gave the balloon-goose a great blow with it. It made a funny noise and bobbed up and down in the bed. Brer Rabbit pulled his string and the balloon fell out of bed in its night-dress and wobbled about the floor.

'Oh, so you want to fight, Miss Goose, do you!' cried Brer Fox, surprised that Miss Goose could stand after the hard blow he had given her. 'Come on then!'

He hit the balloon-goose, who at once wobbled away. Then Brer Fox caught hold of her and lifted her – and he was filled with astonishment that she was so light. Why, there didn't seem anything of Miss Goose at all! She was as light as a feather!

'And I thought she was so fat and heavy!' said Brer Fox to himself.

Then something happened. Brer Rabbit had a long pin – and he suddenly put out his paw and pricked the balloon-goose.

'BANG!'

The goose went pop with a terrific noise. The wind of the big pop blew Brer Fox over. The goose he thought he was holding went to nothing and fell on top of him. He got all tangled up in the enormous white night-dress, and he thought Miss Goose had shot him and was trying to choke him.

'Let me go, turn me loose!' he yelled. 'Turn me loose, let me go!'

He rushed to the window and fell out of it on top of Brer Bear, who was waiting. The night-dress was all round him, and Brer Bear quite thought it was Miss Goose who had fallen out of the window. He caught hold of Brer Fox, nightie and all, and tore off with him.

Brer Rabbit went to the window and watched Brer Fox trying to get away from Brer Bear, who was just as determined to hold him, for he quite thought he had got Miss Goose. Brer Rabbit leaned against the window and laughed till he cried. Tears ran down his nose and fell in a pool on the sill. He just couldn't help it, and every time he thought of the balloon-goose going pop in Brer Fox's arms, he cried with laughter again.

As for old Brer Bear, it was a great surprise to him to find he was holding Brer Fox instead of

Miss Goose. He couldn't believe it. He set Brer Fox down on the ground and stared at him.

'What do you want to do this for?' he asked. 'Dress yourself up like that in a night-dress and throw yourself into my arms as if you were Miss Goose! Where *is* Miss Goose?'

'She shot me, BANG, BANG!' said Brer Fox, trembling all over as he got himself out of the great night-dress. 'Didn't you hear?'

'Ooooh, was that a gun she had?' asked Brer Bear, who was really afraid of guns. 'Well, Brer Fox, that's the very last time I go after Miss Goose. Why, she's *dangerous*!'

So Miss Goose is quite safe now, and she came back the next day and settled in happily. As for Brer Rabbit, he kept having laughing fits for weeks – and I don't wonder at it, do you?

These are other Knight Books

Otfried Preussler

The Robber Hotzenplotz

The Further Adventures of the Robber Hotzenplotz

The Final Adventures of the Robber Hotzenplotz

The wicked Robber Hotzenplotz was the terror of the village. Whatever he wanted he stole and he was always armed with a sword, a pistol and seven knives. Kasperl and Seppel are never far behind him and exciting adventures follow.

A complete list of the *Secret Seven* Adventures by Enid Blyton

1 The Secret Seven
2 Secret Seven Adventure
3 Well Done Secret Seven
4 Secret Seven on the Trail
5 Go Ahead Secret Seven
6 Good Work Secret Seven
7 Secret Seven Win Through
8 Three Cheers Secret Seven
9 Secret Seven Mystery
10 Puzzle for the Secret Seven
11 Secret Seven Fireworks
12 Good Old Secret Seven
13 Shock for the Secret Seven
14 Look Out Secret Seven
15 Fun for the Secret Seven

If any of these is not available in a Knight paperback edition, it can be bought in a hard-cover edition published by Hodder and Stoughton.
Knight Books, Hodder and Stoughton, 47 Bedford Square, London WC1 3DP

abundant, and the more he explored t
coverts the more content with them he be
he had been three days in possession he
thoroughly. There seemed to be no active
about, and the men whom he saw lounging on th
house porches, on the outskirts of his domain,
peared unlikely to give him any annoyance.

On the morning of the fourth day, however, he wa
surprised to note a great bustle and stir before the club-house. From the top of his knoll he wondered at the scarlet-coated riders who were gathering quickly, with here and there among them a slenderer, dark figure, which seemed to stick mysteriously upon one side of her horse. His interest, however, turned speedily to apprehension when he saw a pack of dogs, perhaps ten or twelve in number (he did not know how to count), coming up over a rise beyond the club-house. These dogs looked very much like the tan-coloured half-breed at the settlement, whom he had so often outwitted and outrun. He understood now certain ominous, baying voices, which he had heard several times in the distance; and he realized in a second that now was an old game about to be played in a new way. He himself it was, and none other, that all this fuss was about. There was so much of it; and the colour looked so impressive. For a moment his heart sank, and his brush dropped. Then confidence returned. He sat up with sprightly cocked ears and head to one side as was his ancient custom, and eyed with shrewd semi-disdain the elaborate preparations which were being made against him. Then he slipped down from his watchtower and betook himself to the centre of the most difficult patch of swamp.

marvelled still more at the man-creatures on horseback who followed the pack so wildly. He had taken pains to put every possible obstacle in the path – every high stone wall, every crooked fence, every ditch and bog, every coil of the erratic brook. These, to his light and tough agility, were nothing. But it filled him with amazement to see the way in which the man-creatures – those slim, dark ones on the sides of their horses as well as the red ones that rode in the usual fashion – went boldly over the obstacles. Some to be sure, went down in disaster; and some turned aside to rejoin the hunt later on; but most kept straight ahead with the pack, 'buck-jumping' their way over certain awkward obstructions, and clearing others with magnificent, soaring leaps. Red Fox thought to himself that these man-creatures were curiously different from those he used to know – Jabe Smith, and the Boy, and the long-legged, slouching, indifferent backwoods farmers. He got so absorbed in satisfying his curiosity that he almost forgot the important part which he himself was playing in the drama; and before he knew it the baying pack was almost back upon him. He darted down the densest side of the knoll and ran with all his might across the open – but he was not quite in time to escape being sighted. A great shout of triumph went up from the field; and the pack was sent at a tangent across the field, cutting into the trail and saving a vast expenditure of time and wind. The burst of speed which Red Fox now put on was a revelation to all who were so fortunate as to see it; but, softened as he was from his long weeks of captivity, it cost him too much. He kept right on through the next covert, and across the next open, and through a wide belt of alder-swamp; but when next he showed himself, had there been anyone near to see, it would have been observed that his brush drooped in dejection, and his bright, dapper coat was dark with wet. He halted for a moment or two, to recover his wind a little; then he set himself to try some of his old tricks.

On a fallen sapling he crossed the brook, and ran some twenty yards up-stream. Then, though he hated wetting his feet, he retraced his steps in the water, close alongshore, to a distance of perhaps fifty yards down-stream. This, he calculated, should give him plenty of time to recover his wind and begin the game again as good as new. But that bell-mouthed baying was once more close behind him. He trotted to the farthest point of the alder-swamp, saving himself shrewdly for a quick and secret dart across the meadows to the next covert, and slipped out boldly. To his terror, there stood a group of the scarlet-coated men on horseback, apparently awaiting him. As their terrible shout arose he knew all those elaborate tactics of his had gone for nought – had been so much precious time wasted. For an instant he hesitated, thinking to turn back. But the baying of his pursuers was already in the alder-swamp. Taking a grip on his nerve, he dashed straight through the group of horsemen – who applauded with a volley of terrifying sounds – and ran for the next patch of woods.

When he got there, and the kindly shadows once more shielded him for a little, he knew he must not stop, though his heart was threatening to burst. He feared to try any more of his old devices against these new and too numerous foes. He simply ran straight on, trusting to find some novel way out of his trouble. The hounds were less noisy now, having no breath to spare for music; and this encouraged him a little. Through the thickets he raced, and through a little pasture which offered no suggestion of escape. The pasture was bounded on the further side by a massive stone wall, extending as far as he could see in either direction. What there might be on the other side of that wall he had no least idea; but assuredly, whatever there was, it could not be worse than what there was on this side. With hardly strength enough left for the leap, he sprang to the top of the wall – and dropped instantly down the other side.

19 *Triumph*

IT was in a dusty road winding between stone walls on either hand and stiff rows of Lombardy poplars that Red Fox now found himself. For perhaps twenty yards he ran on, down the middle of the road, where he knew the dry, hard earth would not hold his scent. Then the jog-trot and jangle of a leisurely team approaching caught his ear, and he hid himself in a clump of tall woods to let it go by. His tongue was hanging far out. He was all but spent. And he heard the voices of the pack in the woods just across the pasture.

The approaching team, as it came around a turn of the road, proved to be a big, lumbering farm-wagon, drawn by two horses, with the driver half-asleep on the seat. The roomy body of the wagon was filled with boxes and a barrel, a winnowing machine, several bags of feed, a bundle of dry salt codfish, and a bale of some kind of coarse cloth. The sight reminded Red Fox of the things which had accompanied his crate on the journey from the settlement to the station. In that wagon he had been safe. Why not so in this one? There was no time for indecision. The voices of the pack were already loud in the open pasture. One noiseless leap as the wagon passed – and he had climbed in softly over the tail-board, and curled himself down out of sight under the winnowing machine, behind a bag of feed.

Not two minutes later the pack arrived and came tumbling over the wall into the lane. Fifty yards away in his hiding-place, Red Fox heard the sudden change in their voices as they found themselves at fault. Around and around, up and down, and over the wall on the other side, they quested for the lost trail, whimpering in bewildered disappointment. Here was the trail, faint but unmistakable, right in the middle of the road. And here it ended, as if Red Fox had grown wings and sprung into the air. The pack, being very wise in the wiles of foxes, now scattered, some running in one direction, and some in the other, along the tops of both walls, and also parallel with the farther one. In this way they made sure of ultimately picking up the trail – and failing in this they were overwhelmed with confusion. Presently the field came hurrying up, all excitement. Some praised the craft of the quarry, some cursed the stupidity of the pack; and the babble and wonder grew. But Red Fox, meanwhile, curled up small beneath the winnowing machine, was being carried farther and farther away from the fate that had so nearly clutched him; and at last the baleful voices died upon his ears. Once more his destiny and his wits had worked together to save him.

For hours the big wagon rumbled and jolted on, in no haste; and all the time Red Fox lay quite still, recovering his strength. He wanted to be carried as far as possible from that skilled pack and those terrible scarlet hunters. At last, however, the wagon stopped, and the driver heavily dismounted. Hearing him begin to unhitch the horses – a process which he had often watched in the settlement from a hiding-place in some overlooking field – Red Fox peered warily forth. He found the wagon standing in the middle of a spacious, well-kept barn-yard. About twenty paces away, however, was a garden thick with shrubbery and tall, half-withered plants – and beyond the garden he saw a patch of woods. There was covert, within his easy reach. Noiselessly he dropped from the cart-tail. The driver, a sandy-bearded, big fellow, with a wide straw hat, happening to turn his head at the moment, saw what passenger he had been carrying, and rapped out a sharp oath of astonishment. In the next instant Red Fox had disappeared.

Darting through the currant-bushes and tall hollyhock clumps of the garden, he presently gained the trees, which proved to be but a narrow belt of woodland. Beyond the woodland was an open pasture field, full of hillocks and knolls, and dotted with red cattle feeding peacefully. Very near, however, and straight ahead across the pasture, he saw the mountains. They were rough with rocky shoulders, and dark with pine – very dark and safe-looking; and there, said his heart, was where he must be. But between them and the pasture lay a scattered village, full of dangers.

Very cautiously he skirted the field, fearing to show himself in the open. One of the red cattle caught sight of him, however, and stared at him resentfully, till all the rest turned and followed him, with lowered horns and hostile mutterings. This attention was anything but what Red Fox wanted, so presently, in disgust, he shrank back into the woods, and so out-flanked the pasture. Then he came to a deep, ragged ravine, filled

with a tangle of young trees and weeds and wild vines. Immediately beyond was the first house of the village. So here he hid himself, and lay quiet until well past nightfall.

At last, when the village had grown quiet and most of its windows had been darkened, he ventured forth, bold but wary. Reaching a highway leading straight through the village, in the direction in which he wished to go, he followed it, keeping in the middle of the track, where his scent would not lie. Once a cur, catching the musky odour on the still night air, rushed out upon him, barking wildly. In silent bitterness he punished his assailant so sharply that the latter fled back to his doorstep, yelping. But all the dogs of the village were now giving tongue; so Red Fox darted indignantly up a lane, through a garden, and out across the back fields, still keeping his face towards those dark shapes of mountain towering against the western sky. In a very few minutes the clamour of the village curs was left behind. At last he crossed a noisy, shallow brook; and then the ground began to rise. Wild underbrush was all about him, and ancient trees; and soon he was climbing among rocks more harsh and hugely tumbled than those of his native Ringwaak. Once only he stopped – having heard some tiny squeaks among the treeroots – long enough to catch a woodmouse, which eased his long hunger. Then he pressed on, ever climbing; till, in the first grey–saffron transparency of dawn, he came out upon a jutting cape of rock, and found himself in a wilderness to his heart's desire, a rugged turbulence of hills and ravines where the pack and the scarlet hunters could not come.

Other Non-fiction Puffins

ISHI, LAST OF HIS TRIBE

Theodora Kroeber

Over a hundred years ago a boy called Ishi lived in the foothills of Northern California, one of the last few survivors of the Indian Yana tribe. This book movingly tells his story.

THE PUFFIN BOOK OF FOOTBALL

Brian Glanville

A clear, objective account of how soccer came to be what it is today: the growth of tactics from the old five-forward game, the development of the English club football, and the history of the World Cup.

TO BE A SLAVE

Julius Lester

This is a book about how it felt to be a slave, mainly constructed from the memories of ex-slaves, written down both before and after the Civil War, with a commentary on the history of black Americans.

SUMMER WITH TOMMY

Caroline Silver

This is the true story of a wild pony called Tommy, and the marvellous but unpredictable summer that the author spent breaking him in.

MAMMOTHS, MASTODONS AND MAN

Robert Silverberg

The discovery of the remains of 'strange hairy elephants' that once roamed the temperate forests of Europe and America, was an important link in the discovery of our own past. But what happened to them, and their position in the evolutionary ladder is still an unsolved mystery.

THE DODO, THE AUK AND THE ORYX

Robert Silverberg

Today many forms of animal life are near extinction. This is the story of vanished and vanishing creatures and what we are doing to preserve animals in danger of extinction.

JOCK OF THE BUSHVELD

Sir Percy FitzPatrick

The story of a bull-terrier, the ugliest in the litter, and his life in the hunter's paradise of the African bush. It is a classic among animal stories and is still as fresh and exciting as when it was first told.

If you have enjoyed reading this book and would like to know about others which we publish, why not join the Puffin Club? You will be sent the club magazine, *Puffin Post*, four times a year and a smart badge and membership book. You will also be able to enter all the competitions.
For details of cost and an application form, send a stamped addressed envelope to:

The Puffin Club Dept A
Penguin Books Limited
Bath Road
Harmondsworth
Middlesex